This
Bear with Sticky Paws
book belongs to:
. . . .
KEEP YOUR PAWS OFF!

for Jack,
with love

tiger tales

an imprint of ME Media, LLC

202 Old Ridgefield Road, Wilton, CT 06897

Published in the United States 2010

Originally published in Great Britain 2009

by Orchard Books

a division of Hachette Children's Books

an Hachette UK Company

Text and illustrations copyright ©2009 Clara Vulliamy

CIP data is available

ISBN-13: 978-1-58925-087-1

ISBN-10: 1-58925-087-7

Printed in China

SCP0709

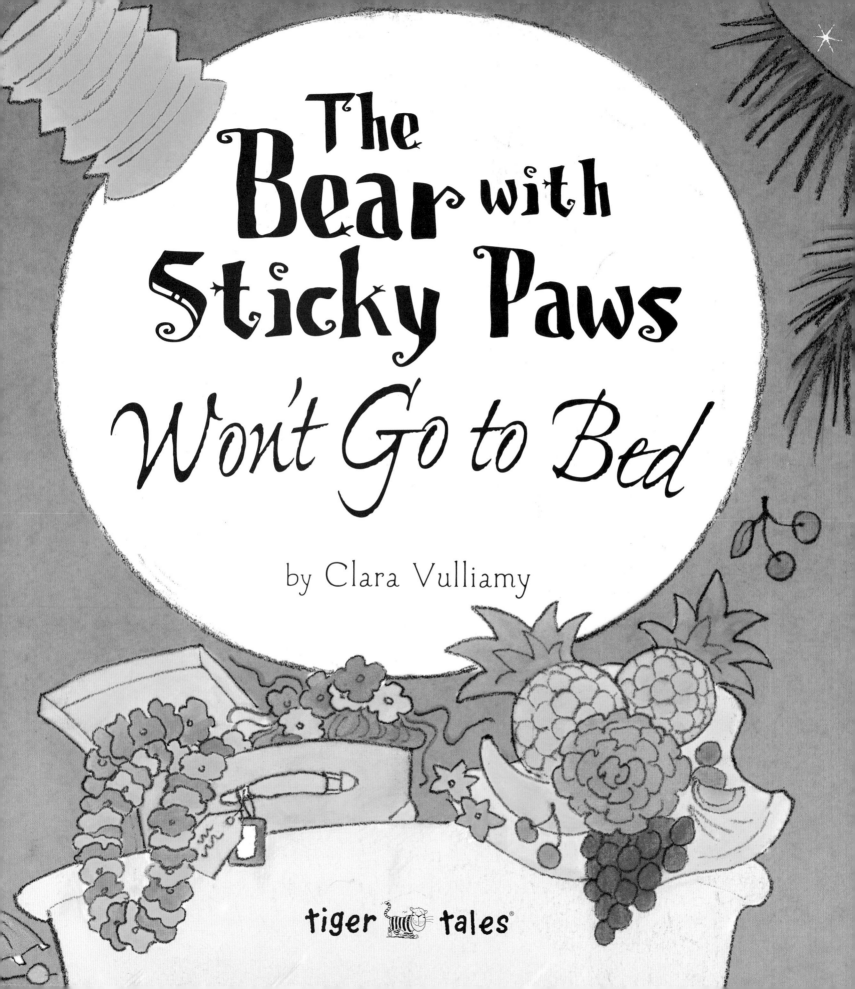

The Bear with Sticky Paws
Won't Go to Bed

by Clara Vulliamy

tiger tales

There's a girl named Lily
and she's very wide awake.
She says,

"I'm really,
really busy and
I'm not going
to sleep!"

"You can play tomorrow," says Mom. "Now I'll tuck you in."

"I won't lie down.
I won't shut my eyes.
I don't want to play tomorrow.

I want to play NOW!"

And she jumps out of bed!

But then, ding-
dong!

At the door is a bear—a small, white, fluffy one—standing on his suitcase to reach the bell.

"Bedtime?" says the bear. "Not bedtime! PARTY TIME!"

Now he's jumping on the bed, standing
on his head...
  "Let's do an ADVENTURE!" says the bear.
  "Okay," says Lily. "I'm not sleepy!"

"ALL ABOARD!"
says the bear.

"Hold on tight."

"HIGHER!" says the bear,
flying up and up, over treetops
and chimneys.

"FASTER!" says the bear,
all around the world. . . .

"SPLASH!"

"The party's HERE!" says the bear.
"Oh, good! I love parties," says Lily.

The bear has

10 colorful drinks,

9 ice cream sundaes,

and 8 sweet treats.

And—oh NO!
Sticky paws everywhere!

"Let's do SAND!" says the bear.
"Okay," says Lily. "I'm not sleepy!"

Lily makes

7 perfect sandcastles,

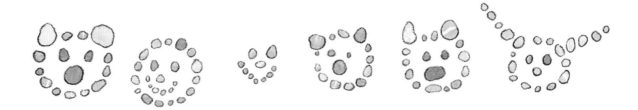

6 pebble faces,

and 5 patterns of pretty shells.

The bear is practicing his BIG jumps,
and—oh NO!
Everything gets knocked over.

"Let's play VOLLEYBALL! I WIN!"
says the bear, running off with the ball.

"Not sleepy," says Lily.

"I NEVER *sleep!*" says the bear.

"COCONUTS!"

"Maybe tomorrow," says Lily.
"NOW!" says the bear.

"PARTY CLOTHES!"
The bear wears

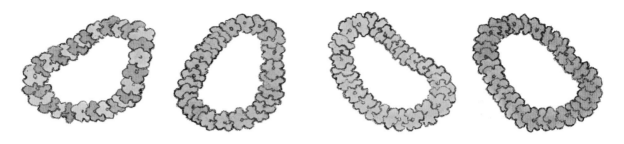

4 flower leis,

3 grass skirts,

and 2 huge hats.

"FRUITY!" says
the bear.

"A little bit sleepy," says Lily.
"NOT SLEEPY!" says the bear.

"TIME FOR DANCING!"

Whirling and twirling,

wilder and wilder...

until Lily calls out ...

"NO MORE! It's my bedtime."

"Not MY bedtime!" says the bear.

"GOOD-BYE!"

The bear is dancing,

dancing away,

and Lily's eyes are

closing, closing.

"Sleepy," says Lily.
"Sleep tight," says Mom.

And there's still time...

for one last goodnight kiss.